A MILLION AND ONE STORIES TO TELL

For assuredly, I say to you, whoever says to this mountain, 'Be removed and be cast into the sea,' and does not doubt in his heart, but believes that those things he says will be done, he will have whatever he says.
-Mark 11:23 NKJV

While the earth remains,
Seedtime and harvest,
Cold and heat,
Winter and summer,
And day and night
Shall not cease."
-Genesis 8:22 NKJV

THE POET'S REASON WHY

"When I was a boy
I did not have a talent.
When I was a boy
I made a promise to God
that if I should be given
a talent
I would use it to
its full potential.

This is why I write.

And when I write
I seek to dispel the darkness
with true light given by
the Almighty.

I am a weary traveler.
A warrior poet
with a pen like a sword
fighting for my Lord."

A Million And One Stories To Tell

Stefon N. Lowman
Edited by Shayla R. Lowman

INk LION PRESS

A MILLION AND ONE STORIES TO TELL

Hardcover ISBN: 978-0-578-52737-7
Paperback ISBN: 978-0-578-52737-6
ebook ISBN: 978-0-578-53070-3

Printed in the United States of America

BOOK DESIGN BY STEFON N. LOWMAN
COVER ART DESIGN BY MICHAEL TOMPSETT
MAIN TITLE FONT DESIGN BY KEVIN CHRISTOPHER
BOOK EDITED BY SHAYLA R. LOWMAN

10 9 8 7 6 5 4 3 2 1
First Paperback Edition

A MILLION AND ONE STORIES TO TELL

Dedication

This book is dedicated to my mother, Joyce Lowman; father,
Neville Lowman; my sisters and brothers; and
nieces and nephews for surrounding me with love,
so I could always see God's face
under these dark gray skies.

TABLE OF CONTENTS

Acknowledgment

I will forever be grateful to Michael Tompsett for providing the cover art for this book.

For nearly twenty years I have been searching for the perfect art piece to complement this book. Michael definitely was a godsend. I have always believed that poetry and art go hand in hand, and Michael's New York Skyline artwork definitely gives a visual depiction of *A Million and One Stories to Tell*.

Michael is a talented artist with a wide range of beautiful art pieces as a part of his portfolio. Especially stunning for me are his paintings of various city skylines and world maps. The piece that appears on the cover truly captures the pre-9/11 New York City that I attempted to depict.

I encourage the reader to check out Michael Tompsett's work, which is truly inspiring.

https://michael-tompsett.pixels.com

—Stefon N. Lowman, The Publisher

Preface

A Million and One Stories to Tell is a poetry book that is designed to be read from cover to cover. If a novel can be equated to a movie shot with a video camera, think of this book as one shot with a photo camera. Some stories are episodic and others are non-linear. Some characters carry through from poem to poem in a given section, while others appear sporadically or as a one-shot. One character (Mr. Willy) along with the poet serves a narrative purpose. Though the book has a dark tone, it is ultimately a story of light triumphing over darkness.

Except for *The Poet's Epilogue* & *Exchange Rate*, which was written in 2019, the poems in this book were written between 1999-2002 with minor revisions and additions done in 2004-2005. The setting takes place in a pre-9/11 New York mainly focusing on the decade of the 1990s and the very early 2000s when New York was a very different place than what it is at the time of writing this Preface in 2019.

A Million and One Stories to Tell also represents me as a poet not as I currently am, but rather as a young poet between 17-23 years old. While re-editing this book in 2019 for publication I sought to maintain the feel of a 1990s New York and the voice of the young poet that I was at the time.

—Stefon N. Lowman, The Publisher

Voice for Many (The Poet's Prologue)

Who do I represent?

An uneducated black man who ain't worth spit.

Who do I represent?

Thugs who tote guns

and sell drugs,

looking for a better way out.

A better way to put food in their baby's mouth.

Who do I represent?

Mothers who cried

for their kids who died

too young.

I represent the man sleeping on the corner

in the cold

who won't live to see tomorrow's sun.

Who do I represent?

Kids who don't think they'll live to see

the age of twenty.

I represent so many.

The many creative minds trapped in the PEN

repenting for their sins.

Lifers praying that heaven will let them in.

I represent the wasted talent

of those who didn't make it.

Give me your hopes and dreams and to the end

I'll take it.

I represent kids with big dreams

with holes in their jeans

from falling on their knees,

when they try to succeed.

Who do I represent?

People whose lives do not go as planned.

I represent those whose dreams are just beyond

the reach of their hands.

Children Of Babylon

Jazz Man Willy

They call him Old Man Willy;
   the Jazz Man.
His eyes heavy, sad and lonely.
Aside from his trumpet,
his guitar is his only friend
along with its five strings.
He spends days and sometimes nights
in Central Park, so they say.
Singing about how
times have changed.
        "Sho' nuff not the same"
Old man Willy,
plays his sweet tune
to ease the city's pain—
and his own.
        "Peace be here soon"
His music dances in the air
and even underground, or so they say,
through subway trains,
up through the concrete
to a taxi cab passing a black man
on a lonely street.
Sweet melody drifts past corner stores
where Midnight's sons gather
with guns aimed

as if at war.

       "Listen, see that life is worth more"

That music hangs on the back of bullets

with vain attempts to slow them down.

Beautiful tune,

stands on top of coffins being

lowered into the ground,

and tries to pick up

the pieces of lost love and broken dreams.

Comforting music,

tries to lift heavy hearts mourning

for lost seeds.

       "Their souls are flying free"

Old Man Willy, they say

is the last of a dying breed.

Old Man Willy, they say,

is the heart of New York City.

The Voice of Babylon

New York City,
that's me– now.

I am perpetual Midnight;
the darkness that has possessed the city;
A kingdom in the spiritual
controlling the Apple in the physical.

New York City,
that's me.
I am where the money is made:
for that reason, many are slain.
Dreams slide off sidewalks and
down sewage drains,
only to get crushed under the wheels
of subway trains.
I have stolen sight from rich and poor alike.
My bright lights and long nights
confuse their eyes
giving illusions of sight, but
they are blind.

I corrupt young seeds
and distort reality
from Manhattan
to The Bronx, Brooklyn, and Queens.
Like a storm, I sweep through the lonely island

of Staten.
All five boroughs flattened.
All seeds lost now belong to me.
Did you really think you could come here to live
without me
touching your kids?

I am New York City
ain't nothing about my streets
pretty.
I am filled with quick cash
whose disappearance
causes whiplash.
My streets are haunted by drugs, pimps,
stick-up kids, and thugs;
the nightly dealings of Midnight's sons.
Better fill your children with plenty of love
and wisdom,
because in my belly there is a beast
and they will have to defeat him.
He in me who devours lost seeds.

Congratulations, to those who make it past me.
Their street education will last them through eternity.

The City's Tales

There are a million and one blocks
and a million and one cops;
some are crooks—
living in a city that never
stops.
Some homes feel like jail cells,
from those homes I hear
the innocent yell—
for help.
Yet hearts remain frozen
though life burns like hell.

Out of 8 million stories, the saddest
are the silenced and forgotten.

In the city that never sleeps
there are a million and one—
stories to tell.

Hell's Men

In dark alleyways
stray cats congregate,
where stickup kids lie and wait.
Watching rivals on street corners
who are unaware that death is calling.

Street corner thugs
are really misguided children
being hunted like vermin
by alleyway demons,
who lie and wait
as dark gray skies turn into night.

Ghosts of the street
never reveal themselves
until it is too late.
They just wait
driven by greed and hatred
from within,
watching their rivals; tonight's
competition.
For them young lives
are like candles blowing in the wind,
trying to stay lit
in the midst of their sins.

However, tonight lost seeds come face to
face
with judgment.

Street corner thugs overcome
by fear;
too scared to run.
While staring into black holes;
the deep barrels of guns—
held tight in the hands
of Midnight's sons.

From back alleyways they come;
night's phantoms.
Call 'em hell's men
on a journey from the pit
to capture lost souls
and take them to
an eternal prison.

Speak Mr. Willy

That jazz tune
sweet jazz tune
moves me.

Sweet melody
sho' eases my mind
and serves
as my eyes.

That smooth tune
moves me
sho' moves me
constantly and effortlessly
through
the city.

The Cipher

The sun rises over Gotham city.
painting the sky red.
Four young brothers stood
in a circle
on a rooftop
and this is what they said:

Hip-Hop is what moves us
through this city that abuses us.
Don't know whom to trust
and rhyme we must.
If you can't
please shut up!
Now, who's the first one up?

First up is Rasheed,
who rhymes about smoking weed.
Says a blunt and a lighter
is all he needs.
But last week, he got so high
he almost died.
Smokin' with Ty
and Klyde
in his parent's ride. But
Hip-Hop is what moves us, through

this city that induces us
and seduces us.

Next up is Ock,
who robs drug spots.
Rhymes about guns and
how he'll shoot cops.
And how he shot forty
people with one glock
and waited around to watch
their bodies drop.
Robbin', says he ain't
never gonna stop. But
Hip-Hop is what moves us
through this city that confuses us
and misuses us.

Next up is Kane,
who raids subway trains
pickpocketing straphangers
and those unwise
to the streets.
A bump from his shoulders
and they are fleeced.
Vanishing like a ghost
into the crowded masses;

the silent plundering

of wallets, jewelry, tokens, and metro passes.

Rarely,

hands of stone and a two-piece

are deployed for those not sleep,

but mostly he

avoids detection,

and for added

protection

he carries a chrome hammer.

Rhymes about the time

he spent in the slammer

and how he hungers for

fame and glamour.

Says he ain't never going back

to an eight by nine jail cell, instead

plans to make millions through rap.

Hip-Hop is what...

Hip-Hop is what moves us.

Through the city.

Last, but not least

is Kyeem,

who chases a dream.

All he wants out of life

is to succeed and

escape the streets.

Rhymes about how he's gonna

get a college degree,

gonna be free.

No more drug infested

blocks,

where kids fight with glocks—

over rocks

in a race to get props or shot.

Instead, he's gonna make a safe home

for his children to grow.

Get paid, and pull all his friends

out the ghetto,

and chill by the beach

enjoying the breeze

remembering the days

rhyming on the cold concrete.

But Hip-Hop is what moves us,

through this city that abuses us

and through this life that confuses us.

Holding us together like glue

cuz all we got is us —

one love.

Pop Life (Angel's Story)

There is a rich girl
whose name comes from heaven.
She lives in a palace
on an island called Manhattan
that looks down on
Brooklyn and Queens.

Her daddy gives her gems,
diamonds, and rubies.
All earthly possessions.
All given in vain
cuz none of these things,
not even those fancy gold earrings—
can ever bring her happiness.

Infamy (Manny's Story)

He promised his wife
that this would be the last—
and it would have been, but
this deal went bad.

Heavy breathing
of a one time hustler
as his feet move frantically, while
running down a darkened staircase.
                    He should have gone out the window,
                        should have used the fire escape.
Halfway down the stairway,
his foot slips,
and he tumbles down the damp stairwell.

He looks back panting, then
stumbles to his feet
half running half sliding he runs out the door
onto the streets of Queens.
Sprinting for dear life;
four pairs of footsteps follow him at equal speed.

He is sweating,
coughing,
almost choking.

His body slows him down.

Mind not wanting to stop, but

his lungs are filled with

too much cigarette smoke.

He slips to his knees

wishing for a moment to breathe, but

four sets of hands snatch him up

now clenched fists;

rapidly punch him in the gut.

The sticky pulling sound of duck tape

echoes down a nearby alleyway

as it's pressed across his lips, and wrapped around hands and

feet.

Then his body is flung violently into the trunk

of an old Buick Regal.

His son watches from his window.

His name is Manny;

not quite a teen,

but like daddy

he has already developed a fetish for the streets.

Manny's mother watches too; hysterical

calling 911,

telling them how her husband

was kidnapped in front of their son.

Police are on their way,

but their sirens ring out in vain.

All while Manny searches for his daddy's gun

whom for now is unloaded.

           Daddy used to call his gun his mistress

           the only lady who knew all of his secrets.

Manny vows vengeance though he will never get it,

but that spark of rage will lead him

to a life

under the dark gray skies

where hearts become cold

and tears run dry.

Uncanny Melody

Through his one bedroom apartment in Brooklyn
the sun shines bright.
Burning away the sweat and passion
left by the night.
He opens his eyes at first light
"Baby" is the first thing in his sight.

Lying in his bed, he is looking out of his window
staring at Manhattan.
Underneath the covers with his lady
touching her hips,
skin smooth as satin
and shines like platinum.

Outside on a rooftop, he listens to a group of kids rapping.
In a nearby park, a mother and her daughter are laughing.
His television is on mute,
news still talking about last night's kidnapping.
Yesterday "Baby," told him that she loves him.
He wonders if she was acting.

After a long night, he opens his window
to let the wind blow in.
The cool early autumn breeze carries

the colors of the falling leaves.

and with it so many memories.

The smell in the air

reminds him of those girls he used to know.

While he stands by his window

he takes his eyes off the New York skyline to glance at "Baby,"

who is still sound asleep.

As beautiful as "Baby" is—

she cannot enter into his fantasies.

She is not quite the girl of his dreams.

Love is such a peculiar thing and seems to vanish in his grasp,

and "Baby's" body is such a beautiful thing—but will not last.

He takes his eyes off "Baby" to look out the window

and stare at the city once more.

Wondering if somewhere out there he can find a perfect woman.

He sinks deep into this thought,

trying to figure out if he is sleeping with destiny.

While drowning in his imagination he is called back to reality.

"Baby" awakes,

asking, "Do you love me?"

Those words, such an uncanny melody.

Secrets

Daddy has a secret.
He keeps a low profile
and tries to hide
the track marks on his arm,
from Mommy.
While Mommy,
tries to shelter
her daughter,
but gazes at Daddy
and knows
something is wrong.

But here is the real secret:

Mommy is sick
and won't be here long.
So she teaches her daughter
 to be strong.

Daddy has been slipping
excessively drinking,
trying to keep Mommy's secret,
but it is killing him.
As they sit in Prospect Park,
Mommy smiles

while holding on to her secret
that she won't be here long and
her daughter is unaware
why her mother is telling her to be strong
for daddy.

Daddy's Pain

Jazz Man's Tune

The Jazz Man sits in Central Park
playing that cool mellow tune—
and the blues
first with the trumpet then the guitar
all day and way after dark.
Up and down Fifth Ave. his
music vibrates the streets.
Notes flow through the air
like a thin satin sheet.

As a hot dog man sells
his goods,
the Jazz Man plays on a
guitar made of wood.
New Yorkers enjoy a sunny day
and the sounds of the Jazz Man's
trumpet as it plays

As the sun set's on the city
and its lights shine bright,
the Jazz Man goes right
on playing deep into the
night.

Daddy: So Tired

Underneath falling stars,
he sits in a bar
drowning his sorrows and
attempting to soothe his scars.
Drinking his pain away,
until his skin turns brownish gray.
The sun is setting on another
day.

You could see it in his eyes
and hear it in his breath when he
sighs.
He's tired.
So tired.
He's thinking about that day when he
will fly—
away
to reunite with his lady.

While trapped in an illusion
he mumbles to himself:
"Don't want to hear any cries."
Tired of the world and its lies."
"Tired of goodbyes."
"Tired of getting high."
"Only want to die."

Faceless & Nameless

She's nameless
and faceless.
She has no money,
her stomach cramps and she falls—
from days of being hungry.
Underneath her tears and dirty clothes
is a beautiful sixteen-year-old girl.
Trying to survive in a cold and unforgiving
world.

It wasn't always this way.
That is before her mother passed away.
Before her daddy went crazy,
and started drinking away his pain
and shooting dope in his veins.
She tried to save him,
but as time passed
he couldn't remember her name or face.
Under the heat of life, love can evaporate.

When money got low
he'd mistreat her
violently beat her—
leaving her body battered
and bruised.

He sold his daughter's virtue
for drug money.
While she laid in strange men's beds
naked and confused.
Wishing mamma was here or death would come to
rescue.

After nights of being abused,
being used,
and made into a prostitute,
she ran away from what was left of her home,
to face the cold world alone.
Nowhere to turn
so she turned to the streets.
The hard concrete
became her bed.
On dirty garbage bags, she'd
rest her head
all the while wishing
she were dead.

While asleep
rats nibbled on her feet
until they bled.
Her body and features worn;
once dainty,

but now she eats out of dumpsters
with hands that were once delicate,
but now covered with blisters.

Time and fate
can be such monsters.

Young girl saturated in shame
her innocence
wasted away
along with her face and name.

Daddy's Pain

She left her Daddy's house
about a week now.

Oh boy!
Hold the arm steady
wrap the rope around tight.
When the vein pops out
stick it in just under the skin—
then let the juice go.
It only takes a moment
now lay back and fly...

He cried when his daughter was raped
the first night.
He got high in the next room,
could not bear the sight.
On the floor hysterical
he could barely get the needle in right.

He told his daughter
it was the only way,
Lied and said that Mommy would do the same.
See,
he lost his job
after his wife passed away

and was not getting paid.
Oh boy,
he was a slave
when a drug slinging
Midnight's son came
demanding money for the much needed high,
Daddy did not have enough
to pay,
so he bartered with his baby.
White lady truly set him crazy.
Dealer let Daddy ride the white horse
for the minimal fee
of his daughter's virginity.
Daddy got high,
but it tore him up inside.

Painful memories don't die
they just resurface every time
he falls from on high;
that false heaven whose inhabitants are demons.
Like their prince, he is falling.
Falling into the pupils of his wife's eyes
then washed out by tears
which are wiped away in shame

and smeared on life's pages
hoping in vain
to wipe away
the sad, sad story
of what their family became.
But it is all an illusion
cuz Mommy is dead, his daughter ran away,
and he is stuck on that brown tape.

So let the brown sugar go
for a second time;
one dose too many.
The world fell mute
and daddy started convulsing,
hoping for peace,
now it will only take a moment,
but for this sin
there can be no atonement

And so his story ends, as hell opens up to swallow him.

The Loneliest

Misery in the mysteries
of days gone by.
Agony and our sympathy
as her tears run dry.
Exhausted throat strains
in a silent cry.
Face stained as if with black paint
from mascara running from her eyes.
Knees bent as begging hands
fill with water,
as rain falls from the sky.
A full moon hides behind
dark clouds
hanging over
a perfect night to die.

Speak Mr. Willy

From the hands of
those night men
a bullet
speeds past my tune.

I wish for happiness,
but they bring ruin.

Caught in between
Midnight's sons at war
under the moon.

Stray Bullet

Gun goes off
bullet travels
like a letter
with no return address.
Moving at the speed of
death,
a few feet above
people's heads.
Relentlessly won't
stop until someone
has been laid to rest.

Next day the headline
reads:

> Young girl killed
> instantly by a stray bullet
> while crossing the street.
> Cops searching for suspects
> but have no leads.

As Lips Embrace

L ips come together
gently touch
slowly embrace.
Weakness in the knees—
As God speaks her name.
Beauty and youthfulness
return to her face
as His kiss
takes her soul
to a distant place.

Tingles down the spine
and tickles on the thigh
as eternal passion clears the mind,
like the sun punching holes
through
dark gray skies.

Pieces of heaven and light
blanket the earth and seem
to freeze time, but
only for her.
Like lovers stealing away
on a passing breeze.
Arms wrapped around

each other tightly
 then squeeze.

In her heart
the city seems to vanish
as buildings crumble.
The world and its cares
reduced to rubble.
When heaven and earth finally meet
face to face—
as if lips embraced.
God takes the breath away
in exchange for
an external name and face.
Her innocent soul
swept away
to a distant place.

Uncanny Melodies

Mr. Willy's Neighborhood

Sunny summer afternoon
Mr. Willy relaxes by his
window.
In his favorite chair, he sits
playing his guitar
occasionally stopping to blow
his trumpet.
Smoke fills the room, from
a cigar he lit.
Quiet for a moment,
but silence is broken
by Jon-Jon, outside on the corner,
catching hissy fits
beating on his chest
cussing cuz his girl Naima won't let
him feel on her breasts.

Donny's on the sidewalk
fixing his car, with the wrong
size spark plugs,
cussing because he can't make
them fit.

Alex is running up the block
with a busted lip.
A-yo here comes Ju-Ju
and his crew—
chasing Alex down

to steal his brand new shoes.
Shaun who seems as if
he is the father of every young lady's baby,
whistles at Aja
while they pass each other
crossing the street.

Aja, beautiful young lady
with a tight blue dress on,
making everybody drool
as she walks pass Ju-Ju's stoop
who's showing off his new shoes,
laughing real hard,
as the wind blows
lifting the curtain on Mr. Willy's
window,
through Naima's hair as Jon-Jon
calls her a hoe,
over Alex's tears as he looks
down at his naked toes,
and past Donny as he runs
after his car as its being towed.

As the sun sets slow, and the
darkness in the sky begins to grow—
nobody goes to bed—
as the sound of gunshots echo
in their heads.

A Slice of Paradise

A hot sticky summer's night,
air filled with the smell of
marijuana.
Two lovers, Felix and Sandra
stand on a corner looking up at
the stars that cannot be seen
because of the bright lights
of the city.
They hold each other tight
imagining that they were on a
tropical beach,
with sand covering their feet.

Instead, they're on an empty street
standing next to an electric pole
somewhere in Jamaica Queens.
No palm trees
or Caribbean melodies,
just the hard concrete
where thugs sell weed,
and police
who stop and frisk
the innocent constantly.

But none of that seems to matter,

as they stare in each other's eyes,

creating their own natural high.

Drifting away—

on a trip past the sky

seeming like heaven

if only in their minds.

As they touch with their lips

and press against each other at the

hip.

Wishing this could last forever,

Sandra holds Felix

with an unbreakable grip,

so the world won't take

him away–

well, at least not today.

So, for now, let the ambulance

sirens be silenced

and let's ignore the violence.

So Sandra and Felix can

complete their love scene

and for a moment be free

for a moment

just be.

The Young Masculine Black Face

Check to check.
Week to week.
Pockets stay empty.

From Brooklyn to The City
feet walk the same streets
day after day,
but never leads him to his dreams.

Just another prisoner
shackled by the groin
to corporate America.
His soul yearns for freedom,
but his mind is not willing to risk
financial castration.

College educated,
underpaid,
black man;
forced into minuscule positions
feeling violated.

He was thrown into the rat race,
and forced to drag a 350-ton,
stereotypical weight

of "Niggers are lazy and can't think critically."

But wait!
He has a brain.
Intelligent words are spoken in vain.
Feeling kinda like a sane man
talking to a world gone crazy.

"And he speaks so well."

Just another invisible masculine
black face,
feeling like a monkey in a cage
dancing for change,
while praying for change.
Trying to hide
the look of frustration
because he knows
that artificial intelligence,
manufactured in corporations
distributed strategically
through globalization,
has already begun to reconstruct
and enthrall the black woman,
so she will no longer stand by the black man

as he fights against his mass extermination.
While black men lose patience,
blinded by ignorance
and no longer see the beauty
in God's most beautiful creation.
In the shadows of corporations,
black love is dying,
as a nation crumbles.

A man can't stand without his backbone.

Unable to stay upright,
he is trapped in a sobering thought
trying to comprehend
the harsh feeling of betrayal,
while he is planning his next move,
causing him to stay stagnate;
working week to week
and check to check.

Clenched fists
poised to fight,
stay buried deep in his pockets.

Prelude to a Glimpse

Broken glass shattered
all over the street.
Pieces of glass that cut
the feet.

Broken glass like
broken dreams,
and bloody sidewalks
like homicide scenes.

Glimpse

A glimpse,
like a picture
that wasn't meant to be.
A single act of violence
brings a man to his knees.
Fists battered,
skin broken
from pounding the concrete.
Man slipping into insanity
hanging on by his disbelief.

Intoxicated was the mind
that held the gun
that shot the woman—
accidentally.
Bullets chased by regret, but
too quick to be stopped
as they drill through the neck
and kill,
but not instantly.
Flashbacks of a lover turned killer
bombard her fading memory.

Gunshot brings back reality, but
not quick enough to catch her falling body.
As the rain falls uncontrollably

with vain attempts
to wash away the blood and tears.
His heart filled with despair,
hands bleeding,
looking at death with a remorseful stare
while being gripped by fear.
Not able to hear
police sirens in the distance,
nor see the ambulance lights as they glare
through the humid Bronx summer night's
air.

Drunkenness, broken by a glimpse
of a reality that wasn't meant to be.
One more shot fired
this time sober
and done for reciprocity,
brings a man to his knees
and his head to the concrete,
where one-time lovers lay
side by side and face-to-face.
Eyes open, but still
as they stare at each other
unable to blink,
forever trapped—
in a glimpse.

Angel Dust

Somewhere on Park Ave.
in a fancy high rise,
which looks as if
it was reaching up towards heaven,
but got caught
between the clouds and the sky,
there is a lonely young lady named Angel
wiping tears from her eyes.
Wondering why
she can't see the stars,
while she wishes on streetlights
for wings
perhaps to find heaven.

But, for now, she
overlooks the city
staring at its beautiful lights
as they shine bright—
but bring no happiness
to her empty life.

She sits in one spot throughout the night.
sometimes smiling, but
mostly crying, while
sipping a margarita, and
sniffing a little coke.
Wondering if her life would be more meaningful
if she were broke.

A New York Story (Angel & Manny)

In the heart
of Manhattan
she sits unhappily
looking out of the window
of her classy
apartment
staring into Queens
not able to make out
what she's looking at
exactly.

On the border of Queens
just beyond the east river
he stands
on a corner, unhappy
in front of a broken-down building
on an unfriendly street,
staring at Manhattan,
the skyscrapers and
one building in between—
at one light from one window.

Their eyes almost seem to meet.

Dark Gray Skies

Jazz Man Part II

The Jazz Man plays
the music of the
streets.

*From the center of Manhattan
radiating throughout
the city.*

Momma's Boy

The years have come
bringing forth the future.
Weeks have passed
and days have gone
by.
Manny doesn't hang with
his friends anymore.
His mother doesn't sleep much
and doesn't put the chain
on the door—
hoping that he will just
come home.

Police sirens, midnight
screams.
Homicide and suicide
scenes.

Momma looks out the window.
looking to see her baby's lifeless body,
lying somewhere on the
street.
She searches for his name
in early morning newspapers.

Wondering if prison

can save him,

and if not

she'll even settle for death.

So at least she'll know where

he is—

so she can rest.

Cigarette Smoke

The snap of the match
and the fizz of a flame
as a cigarette is lit.
Manny stands on the corner
smoking 'til the flame burns
his fingertips
and the skin on his lips.
He stands on street corners
throughout Long Island City,
Astoria, and Jamaica Queens
as beads of sweat pour down his chest,
 from the heat of a bulletproof vest.
His eyes move slowly—
from side to side,
looking for danger, strangers, customers, and police,
competition with friends
who are sharpshooters
aiming to lift him off his feet.
He breathes in—
and breathes out,
puts another cigarette in his
mouth.

He smokes about three packs a day
doesn't sleep much
cuz the nightmares keep him awake.

Memories of friends who are now dead,
and the threat of a bullet
ripping its way through his head
keeps him tossing and turning
in his bed.
His eyes stay open while keeping
one hand on Lola's leg.
Lola is his lover—
a black nine
that sleeps beside him in his bed.
She's his constant companion,
his protection always by his side.
She's the last thing his enemies see
before they die.
Lola keeps him in the business of
getting people high,
which keeps him in a struggle
to survive
to stay alive.

As he breathes out
nicotine-filled smoke rises to
meet the dark gray sky.
Like everything else in his life—
leaves him behind.

Executioner's Gun

L ola spits hollow points
   severing muscles
and detaching joints
of children who talk tough
claiming to be thugs.
Lola blows kisses
and rarely misses.
Kisses that take the
breath away
and sends lost souls
to an early grave.
Then blows smoke
from her lips
and returns to the executioner's
hip.

Dark Gray Skies (The Poet's Lamentation)

Under God's gray skies
an apple wilts
as its seeds wither and die.

In my city, the sky is always gray,
and kids are engulfed by darkness
every single day.
They stand on street corners
acting triple their age.
These little bastards talk about how their
guns spray
and how they make their enemies pay.
But half of them ain't never seen a gun
or heard the cries of those as they run,
being chased by a nine
aimed at their spine.
As bullets spit from her cold smoking lips,
and rip through hips.
Causing him—
a kid far too young,
to stumble and tumble to the ground.
Executioner walks behind
exhaling cigarette smoke,
while the kid turns his head to look around—

and takes a deep breath
makes eye contact with death.

Panic!
Remorseful tears
from eyes with a frightened stare
are greeted by a face of steel
with an unforgiving frown.
Nothing left to do now,
but scream—
as killer lets off a few rounds.
Bullets penetrate the flesh
with hollow points that crack the skull
exploding brain cells
leaving blood and thoughts
now chunks of meat,
all over the cold city street.

In the morning cops investigate
and put yellow tape
around homicide scene,
but murderer is long gone;
far from Queens.

News of son's death causes a mother to weep

knocking her off her feet.

Plunging a family into a pit of grief

leaving a little brother to pick up the pieces

along with four clips

filled with hollow tips,

his brother's old gun to hold on his hip,

and the taste for vengeance dripping from his lips—

leading him to the path that led his brother astray

straight to a coffin to be put in the ground this very day.

"There is always room for one more," are the words

of the grave.

In my city, the sky is always gray,

and kids die in the same way each and every day.

While an apple rots

and the seeds of tomorrow waste away.

Like a long drawn out song

this medley continues to play.

Midnight's Sons

They are the brothers of the
midnight sun.

They stand on corners with
their hands on the gun.

Six shots and they leave
foes done.

Approaching sirens they
disperse and run.

Into the arms of a New York
slum.

Peace Be Here Soon

Far from Queens
vengeance has found Manny.

Cold damp hospital room,
peace be here soon.

Momma's crying
her son
is dying.
The streets didn't
play to kind.
Lola couldn't react in time.

Silence please be still—

Manny is dead
six shots
to the chest.
Guess he wasn't wearing his vest.
Eyewitnesses said, bullets
lifted him off his feet
then slammed him on the
cold concrete.
Now a doctor

covers his face with a white sheet
and a nurse writes "Manny" on a tag
placing it on his feet.

The smoke clears,
while Momma weeps
and the sun shines through the clouds
on the grave of another lost seed.

The cycle is broken.
Manny planted no seeds.
Guess he died too young
being one of Midnight's sons.

The Lullaby

Heavy Eyes

Silhouette from a flame
reflecting, on a chipped wineglass.
Table for two evokes memories
of the past.
Love meets a slow death
in the hands of loneliness.
The candlelight flickers
from each intoxicated breath.
Weary eyes hang heavy
as an old man hangs his head
in reverence of lost love
and missing friends.
Shedding tears
on a guitar with five broken strings.
If loneliness had a voice,
even for him,
she would refuse
to sing.

Not Quite Heaven

H ey Angel,
can't buy that love.

She could never find that love.
and could not separate it
from material things.
She lies in bed thinking,
but never reaches that pivotal moment;
that moment much longed for,
that moment whose image was distorted
behind stained glass windows
in her father's house.

A house built on stocks and bonds,
corporate deals and fancy cars.
Built on cornering the market.
Built on keeping up with the Joneses.
Built on phoniness.
Built on hollow handshakes and fake smiles; misdirection
like smoke and mirrors
that told her that her status and beauty
could bring her the world.
A world she thought
her daddy owned.
Endless space of land,

which brings us back to that house;
built on downsizing, restructuring, mergers
and layoffs.
And she grew in that house with clouded vision
ignorant to the struggles of the outside world.
A world that her house
rested on.
Built on corrupt politicians
giving a blind eye to white-collar crime.
All is fair in business,
so long as millions keep lining Daddy's pockets
to keep buying her fancy things that shine bright
like false sunlight
and fake happiness
seeming to evaporate sorrow,
but making her soul shallow.

She was introduced to coke,
but was ignorant of the boat
that it came in on.

Half went to the rich
and the other half went to the ghetto;
cooked up into crack
and smoked in pipes.

She sniffs simultaneously
and gets high.
High like her home in the clouds
built on Park Ave.
overlooking Harlem
and the home of one of her Daddy's layoff victims.
Who just pulled the trigger.
His body is dropping
and the blood is flowing steadily
forming a pool.
Her house, built on everything is sinking into that blood too—
and it stains the windows
that she looks through.

She is frozen in thought
feeling unfulfilled in a house built on everything, but love
because love could not be bought.

Dead Presidents & The Enslaved

Our people;
mentally incarcerated
by materialistic doctrine.
Spiritually intoxicated
with that pestilence.
That strange disease;
peculiar "gang-green"
that has the world tight
in a squeeze, while
filling the air with gun smoke
from bullets
traveling through the ghetto
to spill the blood
of young ones shot dead
on cold streets
where younger ones wish
to one day be rich—
and free.

Master of modern day slavery.
That "gang-green" lies
to babies, and
doesn't tell them that its path
is like chasing the stars.

An American Dream that never comes true
for the darker than blue.

God of the rich.
Answers all things.
Savior of the poor, but
the love of it is the root of evil.
Especially in the ghetto
and in government legislation.
it's a phantom,
hiding behind luxury cars,
designer clothes, and
charming smiles
with no intentions of love—
only destruction.

It's crack,
turned Hip-Hop to rap
and raped our community.
As we chase the shine of jewelry
it takes parents and leaves a daughter
confused searching for love in another lost seed.
Now she has a young seed,
but she's still a baby
in need of nourishment,

in need of truth,
but confused, so she chooses
"gang-green."
Like a pawn,
a little girl is turned to a prostitute
and "gang-green" pimps her
'til she lays stiff in alleyways
laying in dried blood
spilled from hollow tip slugs.

She was somebody's mother.
He is her only son
now an orphan
left to be adopted by the corner
and raised by thugs—
among Midnight's sons
that he should die young, or
growing old enslaved for chasing
that "gang-green."
Trapped forever and a day in a penitentiary
where he'll recall his life
and curse his memories.
Now a victim of this system's
well-planned conspiracy

to lock black males up
and throw away the key.

Take the strength away from unity
and watch the black family
crumble.
Is this our fate?
To let our humanity be
reduced to rubble
over "gang-green?"

Exchange Rate

A life lost
for 25 cents.

I heard the gun blast.

> "Was it a quarter
>   or
>   one nickel and two dimes?"

Stick up kid
without a gun
died from the bullet
of a nine
lodged between the eyes.

Lacking foresight
a 12-year-old
foolishly attempted to rob
the wrong
midnight son in broad daylight.

Indignant 15-year-old
impetuously took a life.
Now he is a part of the great exchange:
Some change for
the state's chains,
25 cents
for
25 to life.

Dead Presidents & The Enslaved part 2

With the face of slave masters
that "gang-green" takes
our lost seeds, and
those who can't see that
its beauty is really pestilence
stealing African and Latin identity.
Causing jealousy
selfishness and greed.
Shown in symptoms of materialism, while
distorting the truth by robbing wisdom
bringing souls to its knees.

Without nourishment even the soul becomes weak
and fades away.
Leaving bodies,
walking corpses
with no purpose,
but to stack more "G's."
"Gang-green" has so many Black and Brown people shackled
in invisible chains;
being led into slavery—
like zombies

We should not accept
the slave master's reality on city streets.

We should fight back
against media imagery
of our people preaching that our true wealth
lies in "gang-green."

We should wake up
and place dead presidents in their graves.
We should break the chains that keep us enslaved.

Speak Mr. Willy

He listened to my tune
and cried at its completion.
Such a beautiful sight
for my old eyes,
when His tears fell
from heaven.

What a feeling
when my old ears
finally, let me listen—
to that faint tune
that was always there
drifting from heaven like dew drops
falling on
deaf ears.

Lullaby for a Dying World

Etched in eternity
there is an unheard melody
that soothes great misery.
Soft music from angelic voices
eases a slow death when played.
Like tears—
washed away by the rain.

Beneath the surface the devil's laughter
is drowned out by the thunder of subway trains.
The world never realizing
that he has them in chains,
and they're pawns in his game.
But living is not in vain.
There are a few that hear
the earth scream in pain
as the lullaby echoes through
their brain
driving them crazy with its
slow melancholy continuous beat.
But the footsteps of tortured souls are never heard
on the street.
Yet it's their passion
that cracks the concrete.

Barefoot with blood

running from their feet,

empty stomachs guide dirty hands

looking for food to eat,

and a mind filled with wisdom searches,

but finds no future to teach.

Only a chosen few ever choose to believe.

The fire in their soul

reflects from God's eyes.

Eyes that have seen it all.

Seen poor men become rich

and great men fall.

Hitting rock bottom

breaks bones, but

forgetting one's soul

makes the heart turn cold.

A cold heart never hears the lullaby's

drawn out notes

nor the cries from the sufferings'

throats.

As rich men gloat

at strong men with heavy hearts

full of sorrow,

holding up the world with dreams

that there will be a place in this world
for their children tomorrow.
No riches just faith and love
keeping them from being crushed.
The Lord gives strength to those
at the bottom—
and the devil pushes down
in order to stop them.

As bombs rain from heaven,
earth's destruction by man.
The innocent are killed as pestilence
strikes the land.
While government officials gamble carelessly
with our lives in their hands.
The crimes of the rich seem
to go unpunished,
as the poor stand on street corners clinching their stomachs.
Mental incarceration keeps the
mind from being nourished.
As a sugarcoated world is allowed to flourish.

These pictures caught on camera—
plain as day,

which now begins to fade.

Blurred by the tears

in my eyes.

The cares of this frozen world

silences my cries.

As God continues to be the eternal light,

and the devil continues to project lies

that blind the human mind.

The world never sees or hears the earth

as it dies.

While the angels play our final lullaby.

Us Souls Called Change

Fly Home

As the sun sets
its fire radiates through
the clouds.
Mr. Willy sits on a corner
outside of a bar
beating his guitar
like a drum,
'til his head nods down.
He falls asleep,
dreams one last
dream.

Oh how peaceful
eternal rest must be.

Farewell Jazz Man
may your music be heard in heaven.

There will be no pain on the other side
Mr. Willy.

Oblivion

We sit by the
forgetful sea.
throwing in
unwanted memories.

When they hit the water
they make a sound,
but we can't quite remember
the melody.

Children of Babylon

The sunlight is blocked out
maybe this time forever
as the clouds come
toting their bags
heavy and gray
filled with pain
and an endless sea of sorrow
formed by tears—
eroding the shores of yesteryear.

With no hope for tomorrow
they congregate
and pack together tightly
across the sky
casting shadows darker than night.

It's silent and cold
   silent and cold
   cold
   and
   silent
'til a whisper
rises like vapor
from the lungs of a young one,
thought to be a lost seed.

Saying:
        Thought truth lasts forever

         and grows in wisdom's eternity?
But the darkness continues in its monotony.
    silent and cold
    silent—
    and cold.

Yet young one speaks louder:
        Thought truth...

But it gets colder:
    silent and cold.

However, passion grows stronger,
      ...lasts forever...

But the clouds swell with anger.
    silent and cold.

As a dream brings hope:
      ...and grows...

Still, it becomes darker
    silent
    and
    cold.

Silence—
is broken by screams of determination

...in wisdom's eternity?!?!

And darkness...
    silent and co...

The clouds fall one by one
while the desire for truth
is passed along to young ones
and a light shines from heaven;
wisdom's eternity.
Shining upon roots firmly planted
from would be lost seeds.

They sprout
and crack through the concrete.
Chanting:
        Truth lasts forever
        in wisdom's eternity,
as they grow into trees
soaking up the blood and tears of
those deceased.

Young ones who challenge reality
spread their leaves
and reach
towards heaven
'til God drops wisdom—
to kill the weeds

that wrap around hearts and squeeze
desperately,
in a final attempt to silence and bring truth
to its knees. But
the silence can't contain happiness
and the cold vanishes in the heat of beauty.
As the future embraces each other
with words that form a breeze
carrying change and peace,
pieces
of
change
that grows stronger
and forms love, which blows
like the wind to change reality.

Lost seeds now found
form a canopy
over the city
and look up towards heaven
for the dawn.

Dawn

In wisdom's eternity,
the angels spread their wings
in unison
to put an end to a reoccurring vision
brought by the devil
and his minions,
contaminating minds
that they spread lies
like a virus.
Destroying life,
with no cure
bringing death and darkness.

Seated in Babylon
and full of hubris evil rejoices
as satan lifts up in his hand
the skulls of Midnight's sons
and stolen sight—
as he sits on his throne
built on lost souls
to rule over the night.

In eternity,
prayers sound like whimpers
drift closer and
sound more like whispers,
landing in the hands of God
sounding more like cries

bringing tears to his eyes
and words to His mouth
that dispel the darkness
leaving the devil and his angels
in plain sight
without shelter from our eyes
and our pointing fingers,
leaving nowhere to hide.

Satan cries
deceitful tears
before his creator
hoping for his kingdom to be spared.

Guided by God's spoken word
His angels take flight
and drift down from heaven
with chains and keys
to capture their night.

While angelic wings spread in unison
a few more descend
with swords and hammers;
one side blunted and the other like a pike.
Babylon is smashed and divided.
Broken in pieces and hurled down
like fallen stars
over the New York skyline.

Those Who Dream

Rose petals fall at dawn
for us who dream.
To catch our tears
when our souls grow weak,
and protect our knees
when the city clips our feet
that we would come crashing down,
spinning
to a would-be final-destination
that rests on stony ground.

But rose petals fall at dawn
from a garden that God grows.
Falling from a rose white and red
sprinkled
with gold
in a hand of bronze
protruding out of a lightning cloud.
Petals drift slowly
from heaven,
but quick enough
to break our fall,
comfort and mend,
then gently descend.
Holding us tight
as we awaken from the night—
to dream again.

Fruits of Harvest

We sat between the blades of grass
by the river of dreams
overlooking Babylon's scattered pieces
watching Midnight's tomorrow fade away,
taking its pain,
and we wept
tears of joy
and a few in sorrow,
for those lost,
when we remembered
yesterday.

Then we danced
in the winds of change
our victory finally came
and we connected with the soul
of the city.
In attempts to bring peace
and fulfill our destiny.

If you listen you can hear
the laughter of Mr. Willy.

As we few and scattered
carry on.

Us Souls Called Change (call to battle)

U nder the rising sun
    we are the new day.
We have crossed the Rubicon.

Our voices shake the earth
though footsteps are soft.
Call us warrior poets,
we hold pens like swords
dipped in our souls.
Writing truth in wet cement,
while expanding the city with our dreams.
Faith takes form in reality
and hardens like concrete
creating streets were seeds grow
into any beautiful flower or tree
without fear of dark clouds
or the powers that be.

And we,
armed with
only understanding,
wage war against ignorance
to reclaim wisdom.

The battle lines are drawn.

Death lay behind us.

Fear and darkness lie before us,

but we souls

of this new age

courageously march forward.

-The Story
Continues-

After The Fall (The Poet's Epilogue)

We scarred,
       but unbroken
came out of fallen Babylon
with aims to reclaim the city.
We traversed the darkest regions of our souls
and with help from our Lord,
emerged victorious.
Now,
we are poised to fight our war
full of
joy.

We are warrior poets
who shout at the darkness that pretends to be sky,
but in reality
is fragile as glass figures fastened together with lies.
Darkness falls at our feet
broken
into a million pieces.

We bathe in the sun.
The new day has begun.

We represent the stolen dreams
of those who didn't make it.
We raid the enemies camp
and proclaim ourselves claimant.
We take back those dreams
and plant them
all over the city.
Then we turn
and seek vengeance
for the lost,
as we perpetually

confront and defeat our enemy.
God has made us into light;
a mighty army.
Now we pursue in jubilee,
and watch the darkness flee.

We've overtaken their stronghold.
Lies turn to stone
and crumble as we speak the truth,
and inscribe it with pens of fire
then courier it on the wind.
Here we tell the stories of those who didn't make it,
so the world won't forget them.
Failure to recall the lost
is fertile ground for the resurgence
of Babylon
and its many thrones
where satan and his army once called home.

Therefore,
we each speak
a million stories,
but
our million voices
are not enough.
So we call upon you.
We implore you:
remember the lost seeds,
and help cultivate
their dreams.
We will go after the millions
as you go after
the one.

In Memoriam

In loving memory of my friend
Ricky Joharri Gladstone
1980-2005

The greatest poets never write a single word.

Special Thanks

Special thanks to Mr. Johnson, my 11th grade African American History teacher (Martin Van Buren HS in Queens, NY), who made me write my first poem. Because of you challenging me to write a ballad I found my gift. Thank you for making me walk the burning sands.

Special thanks to Joyce Deaton for inspiring me to publish this book after 19 years. Special thanks to my niece Tiffany A. Skeen for helping me with the overall proofing process. I could not have done this without you. Special thanks to my wife Shayla Lowman who served as editor. Special thanks to my sisters Maureen Lowman and Marva Romain; my brother Steven Lowman; my brother in law Carlos Romain; and my friends Ariel Perez and Mable Jefferys for helping with content feedback. I will be forever grateful.

Author Bio

Stefon N. Lowman is an American poet born in Brooklyn, NY and raised in Jamaica Queens by West Indian parents. Both of his parents were born in Saint Vincent and the Grenadines and grew up in Trinidad and Tobago. He is a first generation American and the youngest of seven children. Lowman began writing poetry at age 16 when challenged by his African American history teacher to write a ballad based on *Mother to Son* by Langston Hughes. This sparked a passion for vivid poetic storytelling.

Lowman attended Florida A&M University (FAMU) where he majored in Journalism/Public Relations and minored in Psychology, earning a BS and graduating Magna Cum Laude in 2002. While at FAMU he served as co-creator and editor of The Creative Mindz; a poetry and art section in the campus newspaper, The FAMUAN. After returning to New York City and working in entertainment marketing for a number of years, he left NYC and relocated to North Carolina where he attended North Carolina Central University (NCCU). There he earned a dual Masters degree in Mental Health Counseling and School Counseling. He graduated Summa Cum Laude in 2013.

Closing Argument

Sleep is like the warm arms
of a mother holding her baby tight.
Rocking back and forth
saying everything will be all right,
but childhood lasts only for a season
as sleep should last only through the night.
We must all wake up sometime
to face this thing called life.